A Play

Rosie Moves In

Story by Pamela Rushby

People in the Play

Narrator

Grace, Lee, Ahmed and Jack were friends.
One day, they were leaving the apartment building where they all lived.

Lee

Ahmed, kick the ball to me!
Now, get ready for my "rocket" pass!

Narrator

Just as Lee was about to kick the ball,
Mr Grimm, the caretaker of their building,
ran up and put his foot on Ahmed's ball.

Mr Grimm *(crossly)*

No ball games in the apartment grounds! You know the rules! What are the rules?

Grace *(sighing)*

No ball games.

Lee

No bikes.

Jack

No rollerblades.

Ahmed

And especially no pets.

Mr Grimm

Good. Now, get off to the park and play there.

Ahmed *(grumbling to the other children)*

But we only kicked the ball a few times!

Grace

You know, Mr Grimm sees everything, because his apartment is right by the front door.

Jack

Come on. Let's go.

Narrator

Soon, the children got to the park behind their building.

Grace

I get the first kick!

Jack

Why you? It's Ahmed's ball!

Ahmed

It's all right. I don't mind.

Narrator

Grace put the ball on the ground and kicked it as hard as she could.

Jack

Great kick, Grace!
But it's a pity it went straight into the bushes.

Grace

I'll go and get it.
Hey, there's something moving in these bushes!

Narrator

The boys ran over as Grace pushed the bushes aside and peered in.

Lee

Be careful, Grace! You don't know what it is!

Grace *(softly)*

It's all right. It's a parrot.

And I think it's hurt its wing.

Narrator

A beautiful red, blue, green and yellow parrot looked up at them with bright black eyes. One wing was trailing on the ground.

Ahmed

What do you do with an injured parrot?

Jack

You take it to the vet, of course! There's one just down the street.

Lee

But we have to catch it first. It might bite!

Ahmed

I know what to do.
I'll put my jacket over it and pick it up.
Then we can take it to the vet.

Narrator

Ahmed gently dropped the jacket over the parrot.
Then, he carefully rolled it in his jacket
and picked it up.

The parrot was very quiet
as the children walked to the vet.

Narrator

Dr Ford, the vet, looked at the injured parrot.

Dr Ford

This parrot must be someone's pet.

It's very tame.

I wouldn't be surprised if it could talk.

Narrator

Just then, the parrot looked up.

Rosie

Cup of tea? Cup of tea? Bill?

Dr Ford *(laughing)*

There you are!

It wants a cup of tea and the bill!

Now, let's look at that wing.

Grace

Is it broken?

Dr Ford

No, but it will take about ten days to get better.
I'll put up a notice to try to find the owner.

But this bird needs some special looking after.
If I lend you a cage and tell you what to do,
could you take it home
and look after it until it's better?

Narrator

The children looked at each other,
as Dr Ford went away to put the parrot in a cage.

Jack

What will we do?

A parrot is a pet and the rules say – no pets!

Lee

If we could get it past Mr Grimm,
we could take turns looking after it until it's better.

Grace

But Mr Grimm sees everything
that goes in and out of the building!

Ahmed

I've got an idea! I'll be back in a few minutes.

Narrator

Ahmed left just as Dr Ford came back with the parrot in a cage.

She told the children how to care for the parrot.

Narrator

When Ahmed came back,
the children were waiting for him.

He was pushing his baby sister's pram.

Jack, Lee and Grace *(together)*

A pram?

Ahmed

If we put the cage in the pram
and cover it with my sister's blanket,
Mr Grimm won't see it.

Grace

Great idea! Come on, Rosie, in you go!

Jack

Rosie? Who said it's called Rosie?

Grace

I did. Do you have any problems with that?

Jack

I guess not.

Narrator

Mr Grimm was near the front door,
as Ahmed pushed the pram
into the apartment building.

Mr Grimm

So, what are you lot up to now?

Lee

Nothing.

Jack

Not a thing.

Grace

We're just looking after Rosie.

Mr Grimm

Oh, babysitting, are you?

Well, that should keep you out of trouble!

Jack and Grace *(together)*

Yes, Mr Grimm.

Narrator

Ahmed pushed the pram through the door.

Jack, Grace, Lee and Ahmed *(happily)*

Yes! You're in, Rosie!